ISBN 0-86163-464-0

This edition first published 1990 by
Award Publications Limited,
Spring House, Spring Place,
Kentish Town, London NW5 3BH

Printed in Germany

MR. TOAD COMES HOME

from Kenneth Grahame's
THE WIND IN THE WILLOWS

Adapted by Jane Carruth

Illustrated by Rene Cloke

AWARD PUBLICATIONS

Toad was full of his adventures when he
reached Ratty's house.

"You had better sit down," Ratty said at last,
"and tell me why you are dressed in that ridiculous
outfit…"

But Toad wanted to go on boasting about
escaping from prison and how he tricked the
engine-driver into giving him a lift in his cab…

"I slept last night in a wood and then walked for miles..." he cried.

"Stop!" Rat ordered. "I don't want to hear another word until you have rid yourself of these terrible rags. Go upstairs and change into some of my clothes this minute..."

When Toad came back he was wearing one of Ratty's best suits.

Ratty gave him a good meal, then he said, "Toad, you'll have to be brave. You can't go back to Toad Hall. It isn't yours any more. The weasels and ferrets have got it..."

At this poor Toad burst into tears.

"Pull yourself together, Toad," Rat urged. "There are too many weasels to overcome. The ferrets have joined them and they keep guard."

"I'll see about that!" Toad suddenly cried, recovering himself. And he rushed out. On the way to Toad Hall he grabbed a stick, but when he got to the front gate a big yellow ferret with a gun fired at him and Toad fell flat on his face.

The bullet whistled harmlessly over his head and Toad got up and scampered back to Rat's house shaking with fury.

"I won't be beaten," Toad told Ratty as soon
as he got back. "I'm taking your boat. I'll
approach Toad Hall by the river. They won't
expect me that way."

But when Toad rowed as far as the bridge two
of the weasels sent a huge stone crashing into
the boat.

Soaking wet and shivering, Toad made his way
back to Ratty's house once more.

After he had dried off, who should arrive but
Mr. Badger and Toad was delighted.

"I know I've been a terrible trouble to you,"
Toad admitted humbly, "but now I need your
help."

"We are all sad for you," said Badger.

10

Toad went to lie down after his last adventure with the boat and when Mole arrived the three friends talked together.

"Poor fellow," said Mole. "I just hope Toady has learnt his lesson. It must be terrible to lose your home…"

"I don't know that there is a lot we can do," said Badger solemnly.

"I agree," said Mole. "We are outnumbered by all these dreadful creatures from the Wild Wood…"

"We must think!" said Ratty.

Then all three went to find Toad. When they told him how serious it all was, he burst into tears.

"Cheer up, Toad," Badger said at last. "There may be a way. I know a secret passage that leads into Toad Hall…"

"And I'm ready to bop them on the head," squeaked Mole, grabbing a stick. "All my fighting spirit has come back. We won't let you down, Mr. Toad."

Toad was still asleep the next morning when Ratty came down. He found Badger in the armchair reading the paper.

Ratty had begun collecting swords and pistols. "What do you think, Mr. Badger," he said finally. "We will have to arm ourselves to the teeth…"

"If the plan works," said Badger, "we will be taking them completely by surprise and then we should only need to use some stout cudgels…"

Before Ratty could reply, Mole came in dressed as the old washerwoman. "I went to Toad Hall," he said quietly. "I told the guards you were going to launch an attack from the outside!"

"I hope I didn't do wrong," he went on. "But I thought they would believe an old washerwoman…"

Both Badger and Ratty could not stop praising Mole's clever idea.

"You acted like a general," Mr. Badger said at last. "You have put them off the scent completely."

"They will mount a guard all round the outside and we will attack from the inside," cried Ratty.

Only Toad was silent and Mole saw at once that he was growing jealous of all the attention he was being given. So he took Toad outside, sat him in a chair and made him recount all his adventures — every one…

Toad soon forgot to be jealous as he told his story.

As soon as it was dark, the four friends stood together in Ratty's parlour. Then with the air of a conjurer Ratty produced pistols, swords and cutlasses and handed them round.

Badger accepted a stout cudgel but the others were thankful for the more deadly weapons. When everybody said they were ready — ready for anything — Badger said he would lead the way.

Badger led them along by the river for a short distance, and then suddenly dropped over the edge into a dark hole in the river bank.

This move took everybody by surprise — especially Toad who slipped and fell into the river.

Ratty and Mole quickly pulled him out but Badger was not at all pleased.

Soon they found themselves creeping along the
secret passage into Toad Hall. It was dark and cold
and somewhat frightening.

Toad was so afraid of being left behind that he
stopped looking where he was putting his feet.
Suddenly he slipped and bumped into Rat.

Rat bumped into Mole and Mole bumped into
Badger who thought they were being attacked
from the rear, and very nearly shot Toad with the
pistol Ratty had finally persuaded him to carry!

Ratty kept an eye on Toad as they crept along the dark passage. He didn't want Toad to get them into any more trouble at this stage.

Presently Badger made a sign and pointed above his head.

"The trap door," he hissed. "Now lads, heave away — all together…"

The heavy door creaked open and after a scramble they found they were in the pantry.

Badger drew himself up to his full height as the sound of shrill laughter greeted them.

"Follow me, lads!" he ordered.

Then he flung himself against the door which led into the banqueting hall. At the sight of the battling Badger and his men the weasels and ferrets tried desperately to escape.

Badger made straight for the Weasel Chief as he sat at the head of a table laden with food. The Chief fled and so too did the bodyguard, scrambling and snarling at each other as they knocked over the long table.

Ratty, Toad and Mole all joined in the fight — until there was not a weasel left standing.

By nature Mole was a very quiet animal. The battle quite changed him and he went round collecting all the rifles the weasels and ferrets had left behind. He even asked Badger if he could keep one for himself.

"Certainly not," said Badger. "But you have done a fine job and the Weasel Chief has given his word that all the members of his tribe will behave themselves and do what we ask…"

Mr. Toad was so overcome at being home again that he couldn't speak.

The four friends sat down to a quiet supper and went early to bed. In the morning Toad announced he was going to give a banquet. "I'll write out the invitations at once," he said. And he sat down at his desk and began writing busily.

When the notes were ready one of the weasels acted as postman!

Badger, Ratty and Mole hoped that Toad was cured of boasting and being conceited. But after the invitations were out it seemed that Toad was making up very boastful speeches.

"Just listen to him," Mole whispered, as they stood outside his door. "He's made up a poem all about himself…"

On the day of the banquet Badger had a very serious talk with Toad. "If you say one boastful word about your wicked deeds," Badger warned, "we will leave the room and you will be ashamed…"

"You're right," said Toad. "I promise I am cured of boasting for ever…"

But that night, just before he went to greet his guests, Toad made his boastful speech to the empty chairs in his room and felt all the better for it!

With a giggle that ended in a sigh, Toad left his
bedroom to join Rat, Mole and Badger. They all
looked very splendid in evening-dress, and Mr.
Toad felt very proud of them.

Nearly all the guests had managed to find
something smart to wear. As soon as they saw
Toad on the step some of them raised a cheer.

Toad did his best to look modest.

"It was nothing — nothing at all," he kept saying over and over again to each guest as he greeted him.

Toad wasn't quite sure himself what he meant but it sounded humble!

When all the
excitement had died
down Mr. Toad and his
friends often walked in
the Wild Wood.

"There goes that
famous Mr. Toad,"
Mother Weasel would
whisper to her two little
ones…

Then she would tell them all about the great
battle that was lost and all about the fierce Water
Rat and the gallant little Mole. But when her
children were naughty she warned them about
the Badger. "The terrible Badger will be after
you if you don't behave," she would say.

This really wasn't fair to Badger who was a
kindly fellow at heart and quite fond of little
children. But it worked!